BONE BUTTON BORSCHT

For Sandra, Nathanael and Olwyn — A.D.
In memory of Dušan Radović and his incomparable wit — D.P.

Kids Can Press Ltd. acknowledges with appreciation the assistance of the Canada Council and the Ontario Arts Council in the production of this book.

Canadian Cataloguing in Publication Data

Davis, Aubrey
Bone button borscht

Based on the folktale, Stone soup.
ISBN 1-55074-224-8 (bound) ISBN 1-55074-326-0 (pbk.)

I. Petričić, Dušan. II. Title.

PS8557.A85B6 1995   jC813'.54   C95-930518-1
PZ7.D38Bo 1995

Kids Can Press Ltd.
29 Birch Avenue
Toronto, Ontario, Canada
M4V 1E2

Edited by Debbie Rogosin

Printed in Hong Kong by
Wing King Tong Company Limited

PA 96 0 9 8 7 6 5 4 3 2 1

BONE BUTTON BORSCHT

Written by
AUBREY DAVIS

Illustrated by
DUŠAN PETRIČIĆ

KIDS CAN PRESS LTD., TORONTO

One dark winter's night a ragged little beggar hobbled along a lonely road. It was snowy and bitter cold, but in his head it was warm and rosy. He saw a blazing fireplace and a table loaded with bowls of borscht, noodle pudding, roast chicken, fruit, nuts and a jug of wine.

And his host was saying, "More chicken, Mr. Beggar?"

And he was saying, "Oh no, I couldn't eat another bite."

"Ah, there is nothing like being a beggar," he thought. "Such good it brings out in people. They share. They give. And me? I get a little something too. It's perfect!"

The beggar reached the crest of a hill. He peered out through the driving snow into the night.

"So, where's the town?" he asked himself. "There should be a town at the bottom of this hill. I can't see it."

As he walked downhill, small shadowy houses slowly took shape on his left and on his right.

"Fine," he said. "Now I see the town. But where are the lights? Where are the people?"

He knocked on a door.

"Please, a little food for a poor starving beggar!" he cried.

A face appeared in the frosty window, then vanished. There were footsteps. And then silence.

The beggar went to another house and knocked.
"Please help me. I'm hungry and cold."
"Go away!" called a voice from within.
"Just let me in, for a few minutes even."
"No, go away."
So the beggar moved on, from house to house and door
to door. But no one would help him.
"What is wrong with these people?" he wondered.

He trudged further down
the road. Suddenly he spotted
a thin line of light in the snow.

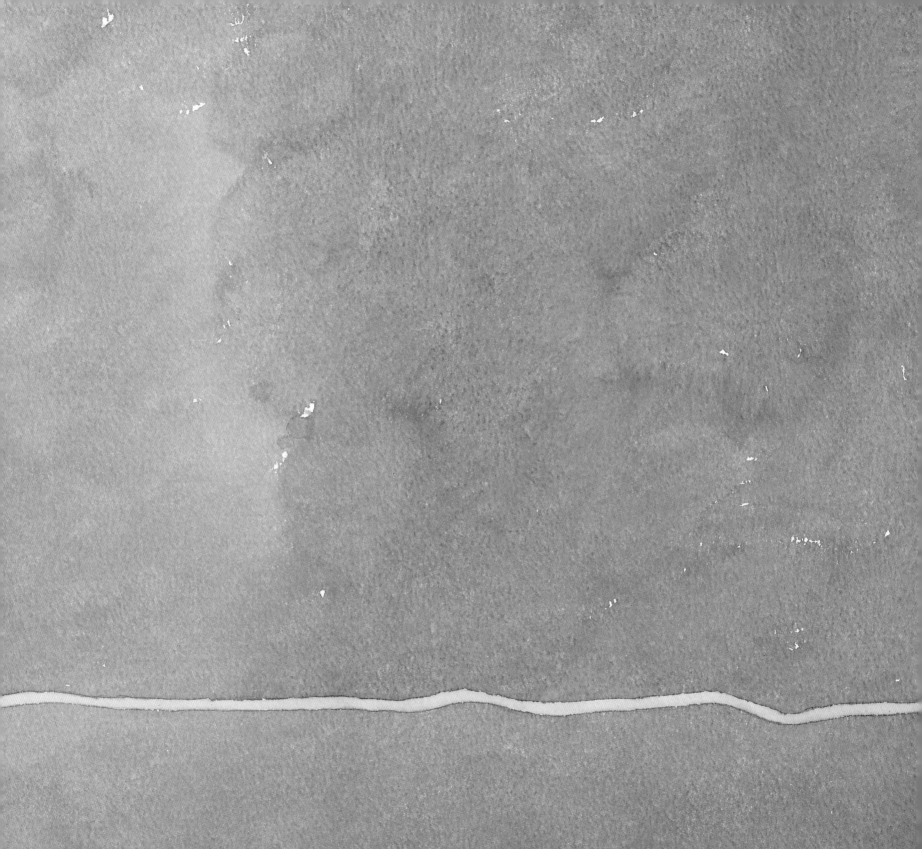

He followed it to a crack in a doorway, pushed the door open and went inside. It was a synagogue.

"Thank God for synagogues!" he cried and rushed inside.

As he warmed himself by the stove he looked around the room. Suddenly he spotted a man in the shadows. It was the synagogue caretaker, the shamas.

"Shalom aleichem, peace be with you!" called the beggar.

The shamas did not answer.

"Strange," thought the beggar.

A glimmer crept into his eye, and the corners of his mouth turned up ever so slightly. He had an idea.

He grabbed one of the bone buttons on his coat and tugged.

Tchk. Off came the button.

Tchk. Tchk. Off came two more.

Tchk. And another.

Tchk. And another.

Still the shamas did not speak. But now he was looking at the beggar. Now he was curious.

The beggar counted the buttons. There were five.

"Oy, if only I had one more button," he said.

The shamas said nothing.

"Oy, if only I had one more button!"

Still the shamas was silent.

"OY, IF ONLY I HAD ONE MORE BUTTON!"

Finally the shamas spoke. "Look, mister, I won't give you a button. Nobody in this town will give you a button."

"Why not?" asked the beggar.

"Because we're poor, Mr. Beggar. We don't give to each other any more. So why should we give even a button to a stranger?"

"Why?" asked the beggar. "Because with one more button I could make us a soup. I could make a nice hot borscht."

"That's ridiculous!" scoffed the shamas. "Impossible! Nobody makes borscht from buttons."

"Mr. Shamas," said the beggar. "I'm shocked! Haven't you ever heard of Bone Button Borscht?"

"Bone Button Borscht?" asked the shamas.

"Let me explain," said the beggar. "These buttons in my hand are very special. With just one more button from you, I can make Bone Button Borscht for the whole town. I can make you a miracle, Mr. Shamas."

Naturally the shamas was very curious.

"All right!" he cried. "I'll get the button." And he ran to the door.

"Wait!" called the beggar. "I'll need bowls and cups, and a knife and a ladle and a spoon. Oh, and a pot, maybe?"

The shamas sped down the road to the tailor's door and knocked.

"Mendel, Mendel, give me a bone button!" he called.

"No! Go away!" shouted Mendel.

"No, Mendel, you don't understand. The button isn't for me," said the shamas. "It's for the little beggar in the synagogue. He's going to make a miracle."

"With my bone button?" asked Mendel. "What's he going to do? Raise it from the dead? Teach it to sing, maybe?"

"No, Mendel. He needs it for the borscht. He's going to make borscht from buttons."

"That's impossible," scoffed Mendel. "Nobody can make borscht from buttons."

"Listen, Mendel," said the shamas. "Give me the button. What's it going to hurt? Maybe we'll have a miracle."

"All right," replied Mendel. "I'll give you the button. But I want to come too. I want to see this miracle."

"So, come," said the shamas.

They ran to the house next door and knocked.

"Leah, Leah, give us a wooden spoon!" they cried.

"No!" she shouted. "Go away!"

"Leah, it's not for us. It's for the little beggar in the synagogue. He's going to make a miracle."

"With my spoon?" asked Leah. "What's he going to do? Use it to part the Red Sea? Teach it to dance, maybe?"

"No, Leah. He needs it for the borscht. He's going to make borscht from buttons."

"That's impossible!" scoffed Leah.

"Look, Leah. Give us the spoon. What's it going to hurt? Maybe we'll have a miracle."

"All right," replied Leah. "But I want to come. I want to see this miracle."

"So, come," said the shamas and the tailor.

"And my family too," she added.

"So, bring them," they said.

So Leah, her family, Mendel and the shamas marched
down the street. They banged on doors. They begged and they
borrowed cups and bowls, a ladle, a knife, and a huge soup pot.
Along with all these things the crowd grew. As it chattered its
way up the street towards the synagogue, others came to their
windows and doors.

"Where are you going?"
they asked. "What are you
doing with that pot?"

And the people in the
street replied, "There's some
beggar in the synagogue
who says he can make borscht
from buttons."

"That's impossible!" shouted
the people in the houses. But they
were curious. So they grabbed their
hats and coats and joined the others.

By the time the shamas reached the synagogue
the whole town was with him. The people crammed
themselves inside.

The beggar looked up and cried, "Shalom aleichem!
Peace be with you!"

There was a long silence.

Then someone called out, "So, Mr. Miracle Man!
Make us a miracle!"

"You want a miracle?" the beggar asked. "I'll give you
a miracle."

"Pot!" he cried. They put the pot on the stove.

"Water!" They poured in the water.

"Button!" They gave him the button.

PLUNK!
PLUNK!
PLUNK!
The beggar dropped in
all the bone buttons.

He picked up the wooden spoon and stirred. When the pot began to steam and bubble, he spooned out some water and took a sniff.

"Not bad," he said. "But it could be better."

"What could make it better?" asked the people.

"A little sugar, a little salt, a little pepper. That could make it better," replied the beggar.

So they brought him sugar and salt and pepper. He sprinkled them all into the pot and stirred. Then he took another sniff.

"Not bad," he said. "But it could be better."

"What could make it better?" asked the people.

"Have you got any pickle juice? That could make it better," replied the beggar.

So they brought him pickle juice and he poured it into the pot.

The beggar stirred and then he stopped. He looked at the people. He looked at the pot. He looked at the people again. Then he shook his head.

"You've got problems, Mr. Beggar?" asked the shamas. The beggar frowned.

"Wait," said the shamas. He ran to a cupboard and brought back a bulb of garlic.

"Would this help, Mr. Beggar?" he asked.
"Why not?" laughed the beggar.
"Mr. Beggar, I've got some carrots," someone said.
"And I've got beets," called another.
"I've got onions."
"I've got beans."
"Would these help, Mr. Beggar?" they asked.

"They wouldn't hurt," laughed the beggar.

So the people ran off and returned with their arms full of vegetables.

The beggar sliced them all. He diced. He chopped. He shredded. Then he dumped them into the bubbling pot. And he stirred that borscht round and round.

"Do you know what we have here?" asked the beggar. "We have a beautiful borscht, that's what we have. A very tasty borscht. Now some people say a little bit of cabbage really brings out the flavour. But I say keep it simple. Who needs cabbage for borscht?"

At the back of the synagogue a woman waved her arms. "Mr. Beggar! You want cabbage? I've got cabbage, Mr. Beggar!"

Before he could reply the woman was gone. She returned with a sackful of cabbages and handed it to the beggar.

He looked at the cabbages. He looked at the people. Then he shrugged his shoulders and began to chop. He chopped until every last cabbage had been added to the borscht.

The people watched the steam rise from the pot. They listened to the bubbling borscht. They smelled the rich sweet and sour aroma as it filled the synagogue. Bellies rumbled. Mouths watered. And everyone pressed in closer when the beggar finally ladled some borscht into a cup. It was deep red and thick with vegetables.

He blew on it. He blessed it. Then he dipped in his spoon and he tasted it. SLURP! SLURP! SLURP!

"So, Mr. Beggar? How does it taste?"

The beggar smiled. "Not bad. Who wants to try some?"

Everyone in the room rushed forward. They snatched cups. They grabbed bowls.

"BORSCHT! BORSCHT! BORSCHT!" they chanted.

The beggar patiently ladled steaming hot borscht into every bowl and cup. Soon everyone was sipping and slurping borscht.

Then the people raised their arms. They rolled their eyes towards heaven. And they cried out, "Delicious! Perfectly delicious! This is the best borscht we have ever tasted!"

"THE LITTLE BEGGAR DID IT!

HE MADE BORSCHT OUT OF BUTTONS!

IT'S A MIRACLE!"

Then, like magic, bread appeared and boiled potatoes, and roast chicken and wine.

The people ate and they laughed. They laughed and they ate. Then they brought out accordions and violins, and they sang and they danced for hour after delightful hour.

And when the last slurp of borscht was slurped, the last dance danced, and the last song sung, the shamas invited the beggar to spend the night at his house. The next night another family took him in. Then another and another.

One day the beggar gathered the townsfolk together to say goodbye.

"Please don't go," they begged.

"I must," he said.

"But your buttons! How can we make borscht without your magic bone buttons?"

"And how can I fasten my coat without buttons?" asked the beggar. "How can I keep warm without buttons?"

So they traded with the beggar. They gave him brass buttons for bone buttons.

Then the beggar left. They never saw him again.

The years passed. One by one the beggar's bone buttons were lost. But it is a strange thing, a wonder, perhaps. The townsfolk learned they didn't really need the buttons. They learned to make borscht without them. And they learned to help one another without borscht, even in hard times. That was the real miracle the beggar left behind.

The artwork in this book
was rendered in watercolour and pencil
on 140 lb Bockingford watercolour paper.

Text is set in Bembo

Printed and bound in Hong Kong by
Wing King Tong Company Limited